Animal Lullabies

by Mandy Ross

For Joe

illustrated by
Krisztina Kállai Nagy

Published by Child's Play (International) Ltd

Swindon　　　　Auburn ME　　　　Sydney

Text © 2003 M. Ross　　Illustrations © 2003 A. Twinn　　All rights reserved

ISBN 0-85953-052-3 (hard cover)　　ISBN 0-85953-116-3 (soft cover)　　Printed in Croatia

2 4 6 8 10 9 7 5 3 1　　www.childs-play.com

Dog

Sniff the bedding
And sniff the night.
Turn round to the left
And round to the right.
Keep one eye open
As long as you're able,
Then dream of the scraps
Dropped under the table.

Cat

Wish for fish,
Dream of cream.
Lick paws, stretch claws,
Soothe, smooth, sleek, sleep.
Hot sun on hot fur…
Purrrrr.

Pig

Dream of breakfast, then elevenses,
Elevenses leading to brunch.
Brunch leads to a late-morning snack,
Leading lazily to lunch.

Dream of lunch leading to afternoon tea,
Which then leads on to dinner.
Dream after that of a midnight feast;
Don't dream of growing thinner.

Ducks

We dibble-dibble-dabble when it rains,
      Quack! Quack!
We dibble-dibble-dabble when it's hot,
      Quack! Quack!
We dibble-dibble-dabble when it's cold,
      Quack! Quack!
We dibble-dibble-dabble when it's not,
      Quack! Quack!

We dibble-dibble-dabble when it's dawn,
      Quack! Quack!
We dibble-dibble-dabble when it's light,
      Quack! Quack!
We dibble-dibble-dabble all day,
      Quack! Quack!
But we dream ducky dreams all night,
      Q u a c k...Q u a....

Hen

The henhouse is dark, and we're locked up snug,
With a peck, peck, peck, and a cluck, cluck, cluck.

Tuck your head in your wing, with your eyes tightly shut,
With a peck, peck, peck, and a cluck, cluck, cluck.

Now stand on one leg, like a good little chick,
With a peck, peck, peck, and a cluck, cluck, cluck.

Sweet dreams, my chick, till the sun comes back up,
With a peck, peck, peck, and a cluck, cluck, cluck.

Cow

Mooooo!
Look, there's the mooooon!
You'll be asleep soooooon.
I'm here beside yoooou,
And I'm sleepy tooooo.
Tomorrow we'll chewwwwww
Grass wet with dewwwww,
And the sky will be bluuuue,
So snoooooze now, dooooo.
Mooooo!

Horse

White foal, learning to leap.
Galloping, cantering, slowing, asleep.
Dream that you're leaping moon-borne,
Silver as a unicorn.

Donkey

Here in our field, under the stars,
We sleep among daisies and clover.
And we dream of the thistles that grow in our field
For breakfast, when the night's over.

Rabbits

One, two, snuggle up, do.
Three, four, curl up on the floor.
Five, six, no more tricks.
Seven, eight, lie down straight.
Nine, ten, bedtime then.
Eleven, twelve, dig and delve.
Thirteen, fourteen, rabbits snoring.
Fifteen, sixteen, rabbits twitching.
Seventeen, eighteen, rabbits dreaming.
Nineteen, twenty, rabbits a-plenty!

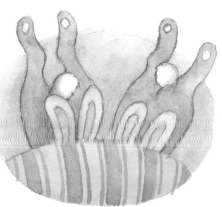

Mouse

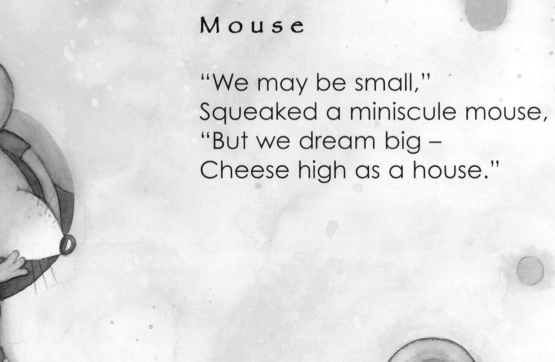

"We may be small,"
Squeaked a miniscule mouse,
"But we dream big –
Cheese high as a house."

Snail

Our beds are ready on our backs,
Built in.
We never need to tuck a sheet or
Quilt in.

Just tuck ourselves
Inside our shells.
Sleep well!

Slug

No shell.
Oh well…
Feeling sluggish?
You'll sleep well.

Frogs

When the bees
Have gone to bed,
And when the duckling
Rests her head,

And when the fishes
Dive down deep
Among the weeds
For a dreamy sleep,

And when the moon
And the stars are bright...
We croak by the pond
In the silvery light.

Nightingale

We are the night birds,
The sing-until-it's-light birds,
The dark-and-starry-sky birds,
The moon-is-flying-high birds.

Then we hand over to the day birds,
The sun-is-making-hay birds,
The dawn chorus
Their lullaby for us.

Then we're the soundly-sleeping-tight birds,
The snooze-in-sunshine-bright birds,
Till-the-dark-and-starry-night birds.

Worms

My little wigglers,
We'll sleep where the soil is soft and dark,
Under the gardens or under the park.
Day or night, dark or light,
Whatever the weather up above,
Wiggle to sleep in our tunnel of love.

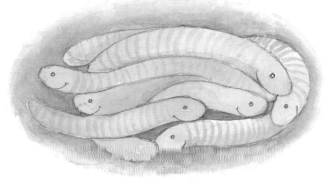

Fox

Curl up and I'll tell you a foxy tale
Of silly chicks,
Who always fall
For foxy tricks.

Curl up now, with those foxy tails
Round foxy toeses
Wrapped up tight
Around foxy noses.

Now curl up and dream your foxy dreams
Of silly chicks,
Who always fall
For foxy tricks.

s k u n k

Sweet dreams, scented dreams,
My little skunkadee.
All's well that smells well,
My little stinkaree.

Our stink's a good stink,
My little pongaroo.
A proud pong, a strong pong,
My little honkydoo.

Settle down, snuggle down,
My little whiffysniffy.
Sniff well and sleep well,
My little smellybelly.

Whales

We're the biggest creatures on all the earth
But, regardless of our size,
We drift and dream in the starry sea
As soon as we close our eyes.

We're the biggest mammals that swim in the sea
With our bedfellows, some of them tiny.
But there's no bed as floaty, no sleep as deep,
As here in the beautiful briny.

Fish

Little fishy, rest your head
Here on our swishy soft sea-bed.
Down in the steep blue watery deep,
Welcome washes and waves of sleep.

Kangaroo joey

All day long,
It's a peek-out, seek-out, look-out pocket,
A hop-it, skip-it, jump-it pocket,
A this-way, that-way,
The-other-way pocket,
A bound-about,
Round-about-the-outback pocket.

But now,
It's a night-time, still-time,
Star-time pocket,
A tucked-in, snuggle-in,
Snooze-in pocket,
A peep-in, deep-in,
Sleep-in pocket,
A marvellous, magical pocket
Full of dreams.

sheep

When we caa-aan't sleep
We aa-aall count sheep.
We count each other's
Faa-aathers, mothers,
Uncles, aa-aunties,
Sisters, brothers.
Over the waa-aall, we count them leap,
And very soon, we're aa-aall asleep.

Sloths

We hang upside down
From a branch, sleeping tight
From night until morning
And morning till night.

We dream of adventures
And frolics and fun,
While we snooze in the moonlight
And sleep in the sun.

We dream that we're dancing
And chasing and leaping –
The things we've no time for,
We're so busy sleeping!

Crocodile

Come on, little crocodile,
Show me your toothy bedtime smile.
Cleaned *all* your teeth?
On top and underneath?
Now sleep long and happy,
And wake up snappy.

wolf

The forest is dark,
The sky is deep.
I'll howl at the moon
To sing you to sleep.

Bear

Deep in the wood,
The sleeping is good.
Can't think of anywhere
Better for a sleepy bear.

Elephants

We eat our jumbo supper
Then we yawn a jumbo yawn,
Lumber down with our jumbo babies,
Then jumbo slumber till the dawn.

Our jumbo snores
Shake the savannah floors.

Hippos

We hippos yawn
From dusk till dawn,
Cool mud wallowing.
Mouths open so wide,
Fit the night sky inside,
Moon and stars swallowing.

Giraffe

Fold your legs carefully, little one,
It's a long way down, even for you.

Penguins

It's freezing tonight
So we gather up tight,
And together up we snuggle
For a huddle and a cuddle
And the winds whip all around us...

But we're dreaming that we're diving and weaving and dancing
Under the ice with the fish shimmery-glimmery-glancing.

shark

Shhhh, little shark,
The sea's growing dark.

Camel

Harrumph!
My little grumpy humpy,
That's enough galumphing
For one hot desert day.
Harrumph!
Time to bump along, clump along, hump along
to our lumpy, bumpy desert bed.
Harrumph!
So rest your hump now, slump your rump.
Tomorrow we'll be gloriously grumpy
For another galumphing hot desert day.
Harrumph!

Snakes

Ssssspirals, ssssssquiggles

Circlessss

Wigglessss

Curves, Curlsssss

Wavessss, Whirlssss

There are even timesss when we sssleep in sssssstraight linessss

Polar bear

Our snow-hole's cosy
When the north wind blows
Across icy wastes
And Arctic floes.

Whenever it snows,
Just curl your toes
As tight as you can
Around your nose.

The deeper you doze,
As any bear knows,
The colder the winter,
And the sooner it goes.

Starfish

Every night, they wait to see
The first bright star above the sea.
Then all the tired little starfish
Close their eyes and make a star-wish,
Take one last peep...
And off to sleep.

Octopus

Octopus babies
Always sleep snug.
The more the arms,
The snugger the hug.

Human

One last story,
One last rhyme,
One last lullaby,
One last time.

Couldn't miss
Just one last kiss.
Now, time for bed,
Little Sleepyhead.